Wendy
Kraus

Gaenslen

The Sleepytime Book

by **JAN WAHL** • pictures by **ARDEN JOHNSON**

Tambourine Books  New York

The full-color illustrations were prepared in pastel on charcoal paper.

Library of Congress Cataloging in Publication Data

Wahl, Jan.
The sleepytime book/by Jan Wahl; Pictures by Arden Johnson.
p.   cm.
Summary: Visits the homes of drowsy animals at bedtime.
ISBN 0-688-10275-1 (trade)—ISBN 0-688-10276-X (lib.)
1. Animals—Juvenile fiction. [1. Bedtime—Fiction. 2. Sleep—Fiction.
3. Animals—Fiction.] I. Johnson, Arden, ill. II. Title.
PZ10.3.W1295Sl 1992 [E]—dc20 91-10176 CIP AC

1 3 5 7 9 10 8 6 4 2
First edition

Good night, Daniel,
from Uncle Mouse

J.W.

For George and Alisa

A.J.

Black Bear climbs
into a soft, leafy den

with the taste of honey
on his fat paws.

He licks the last lick
of sweet, gummy honey.

Sleepytime Bear.

Big Moose steps
out of Velvet Lake.

Slowly the round, red,
rolling sun drops.

On the shore, Moose
makes a bed of twigs.

Sleepytime Moose.

Four Frogs frolic
on a long, bumpy log.

Buga buga buga bug!
Buga buga bug-bug.

They croon a lullaby
to the silver moon.

Sleepytime Frogs.

Night isn't Hoot Owl's
time for drowsing.

He flies over the meadow,
silently searching.

Sleepytime Owl.

Night isn't quiet Mouse's
time for creeping.

Race, Mouse, race
to your warm, mossy nest.

Sleepytime Mouse.

Proud Mother Possum
feeds her pink babies

as their pink tails
swing in the breeze,

on a low gentle limb
of tall twisty sycamore.

Sleepytime Possums.

Rabbit's best blanket
is his own fine fur.

Fluffy ears twitching,
tail twitching too,

within a deep burrow
he snoozes and snores.

Sleepytime Rabbit.

Grandfather Fox tells
each little pup:

Gather round.
Wash your ears.
And wash your paws.

Be careful of this!
Be careful of that.

Be wise. Be quick.
Now close your eyes.

Sleepytime Foxes.

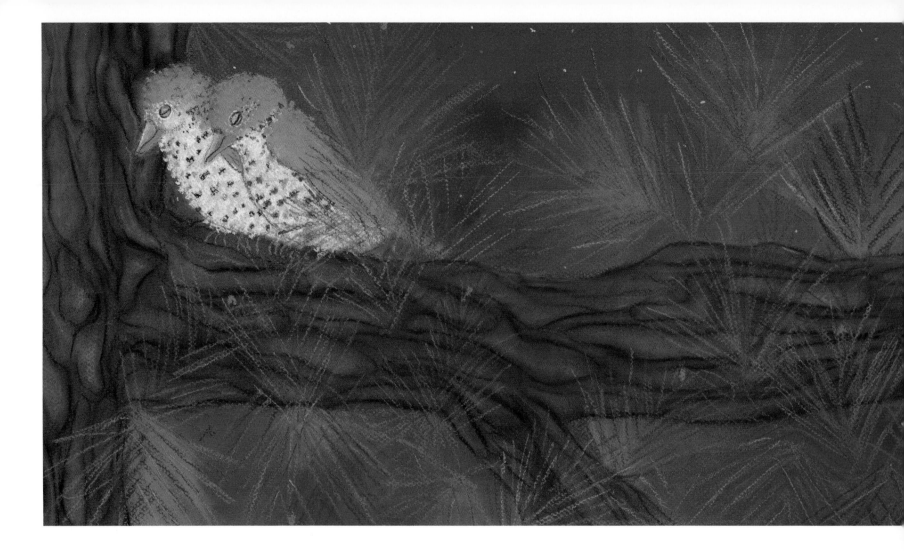

Mr. and Mrs. Wood Thrush
hop to a green place.

High in a wood pine
they cuddle close,

hiding heads under
feather pillow wings.

Sleepytime Thrushes.

Centipede, Centipede,
stay where you are!

Don't walk those hundred legs
in your sleep.

Don't dance those hundred legs
as you dream.

Sleepytime Centipede.

Two sleek Horses,
one silky smooth,
one dappled and dark,

stand straight in stalls
of this silent stable.

Both of them think
about fresh breakfast hay.

Sleepytime Horses.

In a shadowy garden
among turnip and cabbage,

Chipmunk digs down
to lie under shooting stars.

He wiggles and snuggles up
in the warm soil.

Sleepytime Chipmunk.

Red Spider spins
some shiny web

of tiny pearls,
and waits for Miss Fly.

Sleepytime Spider.

Miss Fly remembers
something she forgot.

Fly away,
fly away.

Sleepytime Fly.

On the plumpest cushion
of the back porch swing

old Cat purrs,
hearing cicada
and distant train

until the night
sits totally still.

Sleepytime Cat.

Gray Towser growls—
a squeak at the gate!

Now drowsy Towser
checks it out.

No, nothing.
Nothing is there.
But he had to know.

Sleepytime Towser.

In a small house
upstairs in bed,

snug as a caterpillar
curled in cocoon,

Baby sleeps,
    sleeps,
        sleeps, and
            sleeps.

Sleepytime Baby.